THE
CHANGELING

Titles in Teen Reads:

Badger Publishing Limited, Oldmedow Road, Hardwick Industrial Estate, King's Lynn PE30 4JJ
Telephone: 01438 791037

www.badgerlearning.co.uk

THE CHANGELING

CAVAN SCOTT

Badger
LEARNING

The Changeling ISBN 978-1-78147-959-9

Publisher: Susan Ross
Senior Editor: Danny Pearson
Publishing Assistant: Claire Morgan
Copyeditor: Cheryl Lanyon
Designer: Bigtop Design Ltd

2 4 6 8 10 9 7 5 3 1

CHAPTER 1

THE WEDDING

The heat in the car was unbearable. They had been driving for what seemed like eternity, bouncing up and down country lanes. Only one thing was certain. They were lost. Hopelessly lost.

"What's wrong with this thing?" Lisa's Dad said, tapping the screen on the sat-nav mounted on the windscreen.

"You haven't updated the maps," her Mum cut in. "And poking at it isn't helping you concentrate on the road."

"I need the toilet," a voice whined beside Lisa.

It was her monster of a younger brother. Even at ten years old Lee was unable to go more than five minutes without needing to pee. To make matters worse, when Lisa shot him a look she noticed a thick line of green running from his nose. Lee was officially disgusting. A lanky streak of snot, wee and smells that would embarrass even the most flatulent of cows. As he jiggled up and down on the back seat, Lisa wondered how on earth she could be related to him.

"Mum," he nagged. "I need to go!"

"You'll have to wait," snapped Dad, slowing the car to read a signpost. Dad rolled down the window and peered up at the unfamiliar names.

"Well?" asked Mum.

"Your guess is as good as mine," Dad admitted with a sigh.

The sudden sound of a car horn made Lisa glance over her shoulder. A large people-carrier was racing up behind them. It swerved around their car, the driver still blaring the horn.

"That's Uncle Charlie," Lisa said, recognising the grinning face in the front seat as the people-carrier rushed by.

"Quick, follow him," Mum ordered. "Charles knows where he's going."

"Of course he does," muttered Dad as he began to give chase. Charlie was Mum's brother and didn't get on with Dad. Actually, that wasn't entirely correct. Charlie got on with everyone. That was part of the problem. Charlie had the best job, the best car and – as he obviously knew where he was heading – the best sat-nav. Dad spent his entire life being jealous of his younger, more successful brother-in-law. He probably thought Charlie had better kids too.

"I'm going to wet myself," screeched Lee.

Maybe he had a point.

*

Finally, their car bumped up the path that led to the church. Men in formal grey suits with fresh hair-cuts were directing drivers to parking spaces, but by the time it was Dad's turn the last slot had been taken.

"Sorry mate," said the fair-haired man who grinned through the window, Dad's flushed face reflected in his sunglasses. "There's a lane down the side of the church. You can try there."

Nodding his thanks, Dad drove on, ignoring the cheerful wave from Uncle Charlie.

Within a few minutes they had parked up and Lee was busy relieving himself against a tree. He'd chosen a spot just where everyone could see him. Lisa could see her cousins Abby and Jamelia sniggering and pointing.

Lisa wished she could crawl into one of the graves in the churchyard.

"Stop frowning, Lisa," her Mum scolded her,

adjusting the stylish fascinator she wore in her short hair. "It's a wedding remember. Smile!"

It was all right for Mum. Even after a morning driving around the Pembrokeshire countryside in a boiling hot car, Mum looked stunning. Her bright pink dress was the perfect contrast to her dark skin and, no matter what Dad thought about Uncle Charlie and his brood, every woman at the wedding would be jealous of Mum's figure. The same women would also be casting critical glances in Lisa's direction. She didn't have to be a mind reader to work out what they would be thinking.

She hasn't been able to lose that puppy fat, poor dear.

She's always been an awkward one.

Such a plain girl. You'd think that they'd have been able to do something with her hair.

Taking a deep breath, Lisa trudged after her parents, while Lee scuffed his shoes along the gravel path.

*

The wedding itself was better than Lisa had been expecting. The church was wonderfully cool after the baking heat of the July sun, but the vicar had shocked everyone by pretending to start the ceremony in Welsh. There had been plenty of relieved laughter when he finally started speaking English.

The songs were lively, the bride looked gorgeous and Lee didn't pick his nose.

Well, not much anyway.

Afterwards, as friends and family milled about while the photographs were taken, Lisa had even forgotten how uncomfortable she'd felt in her ill-fitting floral dress. That was until Jamelia had sidled up.

"You look nice," her cousin said, looking Lisa up and down with a sneer in her eyes. "Don't think I've ever seen you out of jeans and T-shirts."

Lisa did her best to smile and muttered a 'thanks', determined not to rise to the bait. Jamelia was always needling Lisa, trying to get a reaction. It didn't help that Jamelia looked more like Lisa's Mum than Lisa did. Thanks to Dad, Lisa's skin was considerably lighter than the rest of her family's, but it was more than that. Jamelia shared her aunt's height, her hair, even her cheekbones.

Cheekbones that, at this precise moment, deserved a good slap!

The thought of slapping her cousin spread a smile across Lisa's face. It didn't go unnoticed.

"What are you smirking about?" Jamelia asked, her dark brown eyes narrowing in suspicion.

"Nothing," Lisa said, spotting something over Jamelia's sharp shoulder. No, not something. Someone.

Across the crowd of laughing guests, on the far end of the churchyard, a girl was watching them.

She had dark skin, nearer to Mum's colouring, and tightly-cropped hair. But this girl wasn't wearing a pretty dress. She looked like she was dressed in rags, a grimy tunic draped over her bony frame.

Jamelia noticed Lisa staring into the distance and followed her gaze. "What are you looking at?"

"That girl," Lisa replied, "over there, by Uncle Tony."

"Who?" Jamelia sniffed, before spotting a chuckling, sunburned man with far too many chins. "Oh, your Dad's brother, you mean."

"Yeah," said Lisa, ignoring Jamelia's tone. Mum's side of the family never missed an opportunity to run down Dad's lot.

"Is she hiding behind Tony's stomach?" Jamelia teased.

"No, beneath that tree," Lisa said. "There, by the gate."

"Lisa, there's no one there," Jamelia sighed and slinked off, obviously bored of her nutty cousin. Lisa didn't mind. She was still staring towards the tree – but annoyingly, Jamelia was right. The girl had vanished.

Lisa peered around, trying to pick the girl out in the crowd. It shouldn't be difficult. She'd looked like she hadn't washed in a lifetime. Easy to spot in the middle of a wedding party.

Nothing.

Lisa frowned. She hadn't imagined it, had she? No, the girl had definitely been there. Standing perfectly still, staring across the guests.

Staring at her.

CHAPTER 2

INTO THE WOOD

At the front of the dining room, the Best Man raised his glass. "Please join me," he said, "in toasting the Bride and Groom!"

Chairs scraped as the wedding guests rose to their feet.

"The Bride and Groom," they chorused as one, except for Lee who burped instead.

Lisa downed the last of her orange juice and sat back on her seat. Mum was busy telling Lee off, while Dad was happily chatting to a distant family member on the next table. His bad mood had vanished, helped by the wine he'd consumed during the meal. His cheeks were so red they almost matched his hair. Lisa glanced around the large room. She hadn't quite realised how many of Dad's side of the family were ginger until the wedding. They all seemed to share Dad's freckles too.

Lisa had always wished she had freckles like Dad. When she was six she'd even drawn her own using a permanent marker. She'd considered giving Lee a few more, but decided he had enough anyway. So she'd given him a beard instead.

There had been a lot of tears that night as Mum tried to scrub off the results.

Lisa glanced at her watch. It was nearly six o'clock but the temperature hadn't dropped at all. In fact, it had got worse. Lisa felt so clammy, her dress sticking uncomfortably to her back. The hotel the happy couple had chosen for the wedding reception was pretty but so, so hot inside.

Lisa could barely breathe. She needed to cool down.

Mum looked up as Lisa rose from the table. "Where are you off to?"

"I just need some fresh air. OK if I go for a walk in the grounds?"

"I want to come," Lee said eagerly, jumping up. "Can we play that mallet game? The one with the hoops?"

Lisa groaned inside. "Croquet," she corrected him, trying to think of an excuse to get out of entertaining her brother.

"Good idea," Mum said, reaching for her glass. "Run off some of that energy. They'll be setting up the dance floor in a minute." Mum looked up at Lisa. "That alright, sweetheart?"

Knowing she was beaten, Lisa nodded and tried not to show her disappointment as Lee raced towards the exit. Amazingly, he only

tripped over three chair-legs and two people.
A personal record.

Gritting her teeth, Lisa followed.

*

Outside, a welcome breeze washed over Lisa.
Lee was already over by the croquet hoops. He
snatched up a hammer and immediately started
swinging it around his head. Lee could make
a weapon out of anything, especially if it was
already slightly dangerous.

Lisa looked at her brother and then towards the
path that led up to the dense woodland behind
the hotel. Lee didn't need her, did he? The kid
had a hammer on a long stick. It was his perfect
day. No need for his big sister to ruin it by telling
him to be sensible and not wallop anyone.

"You start without me," she called over to him.
"I'm just going for a little walk."

Lee didn't reply. He was too busy whacking balls at other guests' ankles.

Lisa walked over to the path, her feet aching in the stupid strappy shoes Mum had made her wear. Still, just being outside made her feel better. She breathed in the smells of the countryside. The fresh grass, the flowers in the garden – even the slight reek from the cows in the neighbouring farm.

She'd always hated being cooped up inside. Even when she was a little kid. Come rain or shine, she would be found outside, playing in the garden.

Lisa glanced back as she reached the edge of the woodland, checking that Lee was still terrorising the croquet field. When she was satisfied that her little brother was occupied, she continued along the path, entering the wood. The air changed straight away. It was cooler, a strong earthy smell filling her nostrils. The sounds of the wedding faded, replaced with happy birdsong and the chirp of insects.

It was so calm here. So peaceful.

Until the scream, that is. It came out of nowhere: shrill, panicked. Lisa stopped sharp, startled birds taking to the sky from the branches above. She stood there not daring to move, her heart racing in her chest. What should she do? Run back to the hotel for help or investigate herself?

Of course, it could just be someone mucking about. Her cousins maybe. The voice had sounded familiar, but this wasn't Jamelia's style. She considered herself far too grown up to play silly games. Abby, then?

There was another scream, shorter this time. Cut off at the end, too real to be part of a game. Whoever it was, they were in trouble. Lisa couldn't just go back.

Kicking off her flimsy sandals, Lisa ran off the path, dodging between trees. Stones jabbed into the soles of her feet, but she didn't mind. She'd been playing barefoot ever since she could toddle.

Mum hated it, always telling her to put shoes on, but Lisa liked it better this way. It made her feel more connected to the earth somehow.

She could hear more noises ahead: a scrabbling sound and a girl's voice.

"Leave me alone."

I'm coming, Lisa thought, convinced she recognised the voice. *I'm nearly there.*

Twigs scraped against Lisa's arms, bringing up angry red welts, but she continued, crashing through the trees into a clearing.

She wasn't alone. At almost exactly the same time, a girl raced into the glade. The one from the churchyard. The one who had been standing beneath the tree. The one who had been staring at Lisa. The same short hair, the same tattered clothes – but now she was panting, deep scratches slashed across her gaunt features.

She skidded to a halt as soon as she saw Lisa.

"Go back," the girl shouted, waving frantically.
"Go back into the trees."

Ignoring her, Lisa ran across the clearing.
"What's happening? Are you in trouble?"

"I said get back," the girl repeated, more
forcefully this time. "It's not safe. You'll get – "

She never had a chance to finish her sentence.
Something barrelled out of the trees behind her
with a howl, and battered into the girl's back. She
went down hard and the thing was on top of her
in an instant, pushing her into the grass.

It was a man, but unlike anyone Lisa had seen
before. The newcomer was short but impossibly
stocky, his arms a mass of bunched muscle. He
was bare-chested, every inch of his skin crawling
in scarlet tattoos that seemed to swirl and spin
of their own accord. His face was that of an old
man, down to the shaggy white beard, but his
features were as sharp as the pointed yellow teeth

he bared in a ferocious snarl. He wore only a pair of rough, heavy trousers, and a cap pulled down low on his thick brow. A cap the colour of dried blood.

"Got you," he grunted in a voice that sounded like someone gargling mud. "You won't get away this time."

The monstrous little man hadn't noticed Lisa, standing frozen in fear. He was too intent on holding his prey still with long but powerful-looking hands, each finger ending in a long, curled nail that was more like a talon.

There was something else he hadn't noticed. The girl may have been pinned down but she'd found a large stone in the grass. Before the man could react, the girl wrapped her fingers around the rock and brought her arm up fast. The stone cracked into her attacker's head and he gasped in surprise rather than pain.

"Gutsy," he hissed, grabbing her arm and pushing it back to the ground. "But it'll take more than that to smash my skull. Not like yours." He leaned over the struggling girl, his foul mouth hovering above her ear. "I could crack your head like an egg."

"No!" shouted a voice and the man's head snapped up, revealing tiny eyes like black pebbles. Eyes, Lisa realised, that were glaring at her. It had been *her* voice. *She* had cried out. *She* had told him to stop. It was the biggest mistake of her life.

CHAPTER 3

WHITE BEARD

"Who are you?" the little man barked, foam flecking his thin, cruel lips. Then he did the last thing Lisa expected. He sniffed, as if smelling something cooking on the stove. Those black eyes went wide and he breathed in again, his wide nostrils whistling.

A grin spread across his leathery face, a twisted smile that made Lisa sick to her stomach.

"Well…" he growled, "that'll put a cat among the pixies." He glanced back to the girl pressed beneath his bulk. "Guess we know why you escaped. Not that it'll do any good, Worm, not when I get you home."

"Leave her alone," Lisa said, taking a step forwards. Her voice sounded so weak, so pathetic, but she had to do something.

"You don't want me to do that, pretty," the man sneered. "Trust me."

"I'll get help," Lisa warned him. "The police or something."

"Why don't you?" he snorted. "Run along. Fetch your blue guards. See what good it does. Or perhaps you'd like to watch while I rip this worm limb from scrawny limb?"

He yanked on the girl's arm and she cried out in pain.

Something clicked in Lisa's head. Before common sense could stop her, she raced forwards, screaming at the top of her voice.

For a split second she noticed the man's eyes widen before she ploughed into him.

It was like hitting a boulder. She'd aimed to shove him to the side, but he hardly budged. Instead Lisa was the one who bounced off, thrown onto her back. Her head cracked against the ground and she tasted copper in her mouth. Had she bitten her tongue? There was no time to find out. The old man swiped at her with a clawed hand, Lisa only just rolling out of the way in time.

She kicked up, her foot slamming into the side of his leathery face. This time she had more of an effect. His head knocked to the side, spittle flying from his lips.

All the time Lisa's mind was racing. How was she doing this? She may always have loved being outside, but was never sporty. Lisa was always the last to be chosen for the team. She was clumsy and awkward, and yet that kick had somehow nearly knocked the man from his victim.

"Go!" the girl in the grubby tunic cried, finally able to wriggle free. Lisa thrust out a hand, which the girl took gladly. Together they ran before the strange little man could regain his senses.

It didn't take long. With a shake of his oversized head and an angry grunt, he propelled forwards on his stocky legs and chased after them.

"Come back here," he roared as they raced back into the wood.

*

The two girls tore through the trees, leaping over roots and ducking beneath low branches. Lisa's legs already ached and her lungs felt like they were going to explode. Not that they could stop. Their short but deadly pursuer was almost on them, snarling and gibbering as he ran.

"Which way?" Lisa gasped, realising she had no idea which way to take back to the wedding.

"Down here," the girl said, grabbing Lisa's arm and dragging her to the left. They passed a gnarled oak tree and the ground suddenly dropped away beneath them. Lisa found herself half jumping, half tumbling down a sharp bank towards a stream. She slipped at the bottom, landing painfully on her hip, but allowed the girl to yank her back up to her feet. As they splashed through the stream and scrambled up the other side, the little man bounded from the top of the ditch, landing solidly in the water.

"Still running?" he yelled as he grabbed roots to haul himself up the bank after them. "I like it when they run!"

But Lisa could go no further. As they found themselves back on level ground, Lisa's legs buckled. She went down, throwing out a hand to stop her face smashing into the woodland floor.

The girl hooked a hand beneath Lisa's shoulder and pulled, but it was no good.

"I can't," she wheezed.

"You must," the girl insisted and pulled harder. Lisa stumbled back to her feet and tried to continue, but her legs felt like they were made of stone. Even the thought of that man behind them, with his teeth and his claws, couldn't force her forwards.

A thin arm slipped around Lisa's waist and she threw her arm over the girl's narrow shoulders. Now she just had to try not to trip over her own feet as the girl propelled them both forwards. All Lisa could hear was the little man crashing through the wood behind them. No more friendly birds. No more joyful crickets. Just the sound of a monster that wanted to tear them into little pieces.

Why hadn't she gone back for help? Why had she come into the wood in the first place? She could be back at the wedding now, being annoyed by her brother and teased by her cousins.

"We're nearly there," the girl panted.

"Where?" Lisa gasped, hardly able to breathe, let alone speak.

The girl manoeuvred them around a tree smothered in mushrooms. "We'll be safe, I promise."

"A stupid promise to make," snarled a new voice in front of them. The girls pulled up sharp at the sight of another stunted figure.

"No," Lisa wailed, as the unwelcome new arrival stalked forwards. He was just like the first man, the same cap, the same tattoos. The same teeth.

The only difference was this one's chin was free of bristles and he wore a large patch over his right eye.

They were trapped. Eye-patch to the front. White Beard to the back.

"Leave us alone," the girl shouted defiantly, squeezing Lisa's trembling body to her.

"'Shan't!" said White Beard behind them, cracking his bony knuckles in anticipation. "Do you smell what we have here, brother?"

Eye-patch took a sniff and his grin widened. "Oh, that explains everything!"

"Not to me," whimpered Lisa.

"The question is," White Beard continued, "what will we do with her, when we've captured the worm?"

"You'll leave her alone," the girl said fiercely. "She has nothing to do with this."

"Oh, we both know that's not true, Worm," Eye-patch chuckled. "She's at the heart of it."

"The beating, beating heart," White Beard added.

"And now we have both of you."

Eye-patch took a step forwards.

"No," Lisa said again, but it wasn't a sob this time. The word was stronger somehow, like she meant it. Like she could do something about the crazy situation. Like she could hurt these disgusting little men.

Eye-patch laughed. "What did you say?"

"She said 'no', brother," answered White Beard.

"That's what I thought she said, but no one says 'no' to us."

"No one brother. Not if they want to keep their skin."

Eye-patch clicked his long nails together.

"And I like this one's skin. I might keep it, after I've dipped my cap in her blood. What do you think about that, pretty one?"

Lisa wasn't really listening to the taunts. She was shaking, but for the first time it wasn't through fear. It was something else, something deep inside her. Something she had never felt before.

A fire was burning in her chest. Strange and yet familiar. Terrifying and comforting at the same time. It felt as if her entire body was vibrating, the blood rushing through her veins, bringing something else with it. Something powerful. Something old.

"I said, what do you think about that?" Eye-patch bellowed, his face nearly as red as his hat.

"This!" Lisa roared, flinging up her left hand. The warmth in her chest – the fire – surged down her arm, shooting out of her open palm. Eye-patch cried out as the bolt of blinding light hit him square in the chest, throwing him back. He flew towards a large, thick tree, his body bursting into a swarm of bloated, black flies as he crashed into the bark.

Not that Lisa saw. She was already twisting, pulling herself from the girl's grasp, bringing her arm around.

Now it was White Beard's turn to scream. He threw up his arms, but it was too late. Another dart of impossible light blasted from Lisa's hand. White Beard dissolved into another cloud of flies that buzzed angrily before dispersing on the wind.

Lisa only realised what she had done after standing there for a second, arm still outstretched. Shaking, she turned over her hand, gazing at a red mark at the centre of her palm. It was like a burn, but didn't hurt, the skin repairing itself before her eyes.

"What...?" she began, "What was that?"

She felt the girl touch her arm. She was saying something, but Lisa couldn't make out the words.

Her head was spinning, her vision dancing in front of her eyes.

She had lost consciousness by the time she hit the floor.

CHAPTER 4

THE TRUTH

Something wrapped around Lisa's chest. Like a snake. In her dream Lisa thought it was Kaa, the python from *The Jungle Book*. She'd loved that film when she was younger. Mum said she would wear out the DVD. She wanted to be just like Mowgli, the boy raised by wolves, far away from his real family. She was always dancing around to the songs, pretending to be monkeys and bears and tigers.

Now she was being crushed by the sneaky snake, staring into his spiralling eyes.

The pressure on her chest increased. Of course, she knew that the dream wasn't real. She didn't live in a cartoon. She lived at home, with her parents. At least, she thought she did. Right now, in the dream, when she thought of home it wasn't their tidy, three-bedroomed house. It was a dark and sinister forest, with trees just that little bit too close together. Each trunk had a face carved into the wood. Hideous. Angry. Howling.

Lisa's mind flitted from image to image. A cartoon snake with googly eyes. A twisted, wailing tree. A nursery with breezy, yellow wallpaper and a mobile playing above the crib. Snake, tree, mobile. Snake, tree, mobile. Snake, tree –

She awoke with a gasp, dragging air into her aching lungs. She wasn't in any of those places. She was back in the wood near the wedding, leaning against a tree. One without a face, thankfully. The air was hot. Humid. Her hair was dripping with sweat.

Lisa tried to push herself up but couldn't move. The pressure across her chest was still there, even out of the dream. She looked down to see thick rope looped around her, tying her to the tree. She felt a tug as the bonds tightened for a second. A twig cracked. Someone was on the other side. They must have been checking that the knots would hold.

Fear setting in, Lisa cried out, trying to free herself, but the ropes remained tight. She kicked with her legs, her feet throwing up leaves and dirt. Still no good.

A sigh came from behind the tree.

"Who's there?" Lisa cried out, praying that it wasn't one of the small men.

No. They were gone weren't they? Blasted to pieces. By her. It all came flooding back. The fire in her chest. The bolts of light. The flies buzzing in the air before vanishing.

Had that really happened? Or had it all been part of the dream, like silly old Kaa and the forest of faces?

Lisa strained against her bonds as whoever had tied her up walked slowly around the tree.

"You," she breathed as the person came to a stop in front of her.

"Hi," the girl in the tattered tunic said. "Sorry about the ropes."

"Sorry?" Lisa repeated, not quite believing what she was hearing. "What are you doing?"

The girl looked sad. "What's necessary," she said, avoiding Lisa's eyes.

"I tried to help you," Lisa said, anger filling her voice. "Against those..." she searched for the right word, "against those men."

"They're not men," the girl said, crouching down on her haunches and picking up a stick. She examined it closely, anything not to face Lisa.

"Then what are they?"

"Redcaps," came the reply, although Lisa was still none the wiser.

"What?"

"You know," the girl said, picking a bit of bark from the stick with a dirty thumbnail. "Gnomes."

Lisa snorted. Tied up against a tree or not, she'd never heard anything so ridiculous. "Gnomes? Like those little ornaments people put in their gardens? Pointy hats and fishing rods?"

Her Nan used to have gnomes by her greenhouse. Funny little things. Lee had smashed them while playing football. Mum had been furious.

The girl looked up, finally meeting Lisa's gaze. There was a strange look in her eyes. Regret? Resentment? Lisa couldn't tell.

"I wouldn't know," the girl said. "I've never been in a garden, have I?"

"How would I know?" replied Lisa. Nothing about this made sense. *Have I gone mad?* Lisa thought. Maybe. It would at least explain the girl and the Redcaps and the lights that burst from her hands.

"It's funny though," said the girl.

"What is?"

"I've hated you for years, and yet I tried to save you from the Redcaps." She looked at Lisa again. "Why would I do that?"

Lisa had questions of her own. "You hated me? Why? What have I done to you?"

A wry smile flickered over the girl's grubby face.

"You stole my life."

Yeah. Lisa had gone officially insane.

In front of her the girl sat down, crossing her legs.

"You have no idea, do you?" she said, examining Lisa's face as closely as she had the stick. "You have no idea who you are?"

"I'm Lisa," Lisa said, hoping that would clear up the confusion. "Lisa Frick. I was at a wedding..."

The girl repeated Lisa's name, rolling it around her tongue. "Lisa. Lisa. Lisa. So that's what they called me."

"Who?"

"My parents."

"Where are they?" asked Lisa.

"Back at the wedding," the girl said coldly. "With my little brother, Lee."

Lee? What was the freak talking about now?

The girl settled back. "Have you ever heard of a Changeling?"

Lisa didn't think so. She wasn't sure of anything any more. She shook her head anyway.

"They're fairies, left in the place of human infants. Used to happen loads in the old days, apparently. Not so much now."

Lisa wasn't following any of this. Fairies? It had to be a joke. "So, what happens to the babies?" she asked, not thinking for a minute that she'd understand the answer.

The girl's mouth set into a grim line. "Stolen. Taken back to the fairy kingdom, never to see the human world again. The Changeling grows up in their place. A cuckoo in the nest."

"Are you saying that's what happened to you?" Lisa asked, desperately trying to make sense of the weirdest conversation she'd ever had.

"Look at me," the girl said in reply. "*Really* look at me. Remind you of anyone?"

Lisa did what she was told, realisation finally dawning. Her heart felt like it missed a beat. The skin tone, darker than Lisa's own. More like her Mum's skin. And her brother's. And those eyes, that hair − even cut short.

The freckles on her face.

"You were my Changeling," the girl said softly. "You were placed in my crib when the fairies came for me. You took my life. Took my name."

"No," Lisa said, shaking her head. "That's not possible."

"Isn't it?" the girl asked, raising an eyebrow. Even that gesture was familiar. Lisa's Mum did it every time she was making a point. "Have you ever felt like you don't belong, that you don't quite fit in? Not like the others. Not like your Mum, your Dad, your little brother."

Lisa couldn't speak, her voice catching in her throat.

The girl stood and looked down at her, a look of pure hatred on her face.

"You stole my life, and now I'm taking it back."

CHAPTER 5

CUCKOOS

"This is crazy," Lisa said, struggling against the ropes. "You've got to let me go."

The girl now seemed to be ignoring her, walking around the tree in circles. Every few steps she dropped flower petals to form a large ring with Lisa in the centre.

Lisa tried a different approach. "So, if you were supposed to have lived my life, what's your name?"

"Worm," came the muttered reply.

"Worm?" Lisa repeated.

"That's what they've always called me," Worm said. "Ever since I was a baby. You've no idea what it's like…"

"In the fairy kingdom?"

Worm nodded. "They've made me work all my life. I've had to look after them, day and night. 'Do this, Worm. Scrub that.' And all this time, you've been in my house, with my family."

Lisa didn't want to go through that again. There were other questions to ask. "Those lights from my hands?" she asked. "What were they?"

Worm stopped and looked at her. When she finally spoke, her nose wrinkled as if she'd smelled something disgusting. "Your magic. You're one of them."

"A fairy?"

"They call themselves the Faye, although there's all different kinds. Elves. Goblins," she paused, "Redcaps."

A haunted look passed over Worm's face. "They're the worst of all. Sadists the lot of them. They live to bring pain. Do you know why they're called Redcaps, Lisa? Do you know how they get their name?"

Lisa shook her head. Of course she didn't. This was all insane.

"Those hats they wear," Worm explained. "They dye them in the blood of their victims. And they're never given a chance to dry out. New blood every day."

The pieces of the puzzle started to fall together. "The Redcap who attacked you in the wood," Lisa said. "It was trying to take you back. To the fairy kingdom."

Worm nodded, rubbing the back of her neck. "They knew I was coming after you."

"Then why did you help me? Why did you run with me?"

Worm shrugged. "I honestly don't know. I should have let them take you there and then, but..."

"You couldn't," Lisa prompted, seeing her chance. "You couldn't let them hurt me. Because you're kind, under all that anger. You care."

"I've got every right to be angry," Worm snapped.

"Maybe I can help you," Lisa said, forcing sympathy into her voice.

"Help me?" asked Worm, her voice suddenly unsure. "How?"

Something moved in the trees, cutting the conversation short.

"What was that?" Lisa asked. "The Redcaps?"

Worm peered into the shadows between the trees. "They'll come back in force, especially now

that you've used your magic and killed
their brothers."

"And that's why you've tied me up," said Lisa,
everything finally clear. "So they find me and not
you. So you can go home, to my..." she stopped
herself, "to your parents."

There were more noises. Branches rustling.
Shouts – not as far away as Lisa would have liked.

"Yeah," said Worm. "That's right." She didn't
sound so sure any more.

"But what then?" Lisa asked. "You can't just
walk up to Mum and Dad and demand they
take you back. They don't know you. They think
I'm their daughter. How on earth are you going
to persuade them to accept you? *You'll* be the
cuckoo in the nest this time."

Worm ran a hand through her hair. "I don't
know. I never thought I'd get this far to be
honest." The voices were getting nearer now.

Deep. Harsh. "I'll work something out when I get there."

"We could work it out together?" Lisa suggested.

Worm turned back to her. "What do you mean?"

"What I said. I can help you try to explain all this. Whether I'm their daughter or not, they know me. They brought me up. Perhaps together we can make them understand."

Lisa fell quiet, waiting for Worm to make her decision. The girl stood there for a moment, obviously going over and over the conversation in her head.

They could make out words in the woodland now: "Pretties, pretties, pretties. Where are you?"

"Or you could just take a chance," Lisa said hurriedly. "Stroll up at the wedding and say 'Hi Mum and Dad. I'm your real daughter. Forget about the other one.' I'm sure that'll work."

Worm glared at her for a moment, before ducking back behind the tree. The Redcaps were so close that Lisa could almost smell them. Stale sweat and blood.

"Pretties, pretties, pretties..."

The ropes around her chest loosened and Lisa shrugged herself free. Worm appeared back beside her, holding out her hand just as Lisa had in the clearing.

"Come on then. If we're going to do this, let's do it now."

Lisa jumped to her feet, ignoring the aches in her arms and legs. "Which way is the hotel?" she asked.

Worm looked confused.

"The big house," Lisa explained.

"Through here," Worm said, grasping Lisa's hand and leading her forwards.

By the time the Redcaps found the tree and the ring of flowers moments later, the girls had vanished.

CHAPTER 6

SURROUNDED

For the second time that day the girls ran, but this time Lisa wasn't scared. Now she knew what she was running from and why. Everything Worm said had made sense. Don't ask her how, but she knew that the girl was telling the truth. It was as if the final piece of the puzzle had snapped into place. All the questions she'd ever had, answered. The way she felt about herself and her family.

Finally, she knew who she was and she knew what she had to do.

"Through these trees to the left," Worm urged, still pulling Lisa forwards. "The big house is straight ahead from that point."

"Are you sure?"

"Of course I am."

Lisa squeezed her hand. "Thank you for trusting me," she said, but Worm didn't look back.

"Do I have any choice?" she said as they rounded the trees. Worm let out a gasp and came to a stop, Lisa barging into her.

"What are you doing?" Lisa asked.

Worm didn't reply. She didn't have to. A line of Redcaps stood in front of them, a leer on each and every wrinkled face.

"Quick," Lisa said, pulling Worm in the other direction. "Back the way we came."

It was too late. The Redcaps were behind them too, while even more moved in from the trees to the side.

They were surrounded.

The two girls stood back-to-back, eyes darting from one gnome to another.

"Well, well, well," said a Redcap with a huge, bushy moustache. He was taller than the others, bulkier too. Lisa guessed he was their leader. "You've led us a merry dance," he said. "Both of you."

"I'm not going back," Worm shouted, her voice cracking with fear. "You can't make me."

"It's you or her," the Redcap said. "Our orders are to bring a girl back with us. We don't care which one, do we brothers?"

The Redcaps let out a cheer, clicking their nails together.

Lisa felt Worm tense behind her. "You can't hurt me," the girl said. "I'm not on my own any more. I'm not your Worm. I have a family."

Lisa didn't say anything. She just felt the fire burn in her belly, ready to burst out.

"A family, she says," the Redcap crowed. "Do you hear that, brothers? The worm has a family. Shall we send her back to them, limb by limb?"

More cheers and cackles filled the wood, frightening away what was left of the wildlife. Somehow Lisa could feel them leave. The birds in the sky above, the mice scurrying through the undergrowth. She could even sense the spiders scuttling away as fast as their legs could carry them. They didn't want to see this.

No one did.

The heat swelled in Lisa's chest.

"Enough of this," the Redcap leader said. "My hat's feeling dry and we have a job to do, ain't that right, lads?"

"Then what are you waiting for?" Worm shouted back defiantly. "My sister banished your brothers, she can do the same to you!"

Sister? thought Lisa. Is that really what they were?

As one, the Redcaps screeched in triumph and ran towards the girls, ready to harvest fresh blood for their hats.

"Lisa," Worm cried, "whatever you're planning, do it now!"

Closing her eyes, Lisa clapped her hands together.

The wood was bathed in the light of a thousand suns.

*

Worm had never experienced anything like it. Not even when she crossed the boundary between the fairy and human worlds. It had been painful, like her soul was being pulled in two, but being caught in the middle of Lisa's magic? Nothing could describe that.

The only comfort was what the unnatural light must have done to the Redcaps. She could hear them groaning all around. She hoped that they were as disorientated as she was. That their muscles burned half as much.

They deserved it, and much, much more.

Still, she was surprised that they hadn't been torn apart, like White Beard and Eye-patch. Perhaps Lisa had used a different spell. Maybe she was learning to control her powers.

"L-Lisa," Worm croaked, her throat parched. "We need to go."

She staggered to her feet, her eyes still recovering. She could see shapes on the ground around her.

Some were rolling about in pain, others were slumped over. They had to be the Redcaps.

"Lisa!" She reached out, groping blindly but finding nothing but air. "Lisa, where are you?"

"Gone," rumbled a voice. The leader of the pack. She spun around to face him, her eyes finally able to focus. All around, the Redcaps were picking themselves up, glowering at her.

She whirled about, looking for Lisa, but the Changeling was nowhere to be seen.

"No," Worm whimpered. "No, she can't have..."

"Can't have left you?" mimicked the Redcap. "Can't have abandoned you as soon as possible?"

Worm felt all the strength drain from her body. She sank down on her knees, sobs already bubbling from her chest. "She wouldn't. She said..."

The tears flowed freely. Tears of disappointment more than anger. Of inevitability.

"Get her!" the Redcap screamed and the pack leaped forwards.

If anyone had been watching they would have seen the gnomes swarm over the crying girl. They would have heard them snarl and cheer and roar.

And then they would have seen the air shimmer, snatching the writhing mass of bodies from sight. There one minute, gone the next, leaving nothing behind.

*

"There you are," Mum snapped as Lisa tottered down the path from the wood. "Where have you been? Your father and I have been worried sick."

Nearby, Lee shouted, "Dad! Mum's found her. She was in the wood!"

Dad came running, his face like a beetroot. "Lisa! Where did you go?"

"And what on earth have you been doing?" Mum said, brushing at the mud on Lisa's dress. "Look at the state of you."

"Sorry, Mum," Lisa said, looking at the ground. "I went for a walk and fell down a bank."

"Are you hurt?" Dad asked.

Lisa shook her head. "Don't think so."

"We're going to have to take her back home," Mum said to Dad, barely keeping her anger in check. "She can't stay here, looking like that. It's embarrassing."

Behind the adults, Lee whooped and punched the air. Lisa shared a secret smile with him. Anything to get as far away from this place as possible.

"And don't think this is over, young lady," Mum continued as she bustled them over to the car park. "Sometimes I wonder how I produced a girl like you."

Lisa grinned. She didn't mind Mum ranting and raving. She didn't even mind the lecture that was sure to last the entire journey.

None of that mattered.

She was going home.

Where she belonged.

THE END